# BABAR
## Goes to School

Abrams Books for Young Readers
New York

Babar and Celeste were having a very busy day. They had papers to sign, letters to write, and important decisions to make. They stayed in their study, working and working.

Meanwhile, Pom, Flora, Alexander, and Isabelle were playing right outside the window.

"I have it!" shouted Flora.

"No, I have it!" Alexander yelled.

"Give it to me!" Isabelle chimed in.

*Thump, thump, thump* went the ball as it bounced against the wall of the house.

Finally, Babar could no longer stand the noise. He got up from his desk and went outside. "You children simply must be quieter!" he called to them. "I am working very hard! It's not an easy job to be a grown-up, you know!"

"Sorry," said the children. "We'll be quieter."

"They do need to run and play sometimes, though," said Celeste.

"It's true," said Pom. "We do need to run and play. Sometimes it's not easy to be a child, either."

Babar was surprised. "Not easy to be a child?" he said. "What is it that's not easy?"

"Well," said Pom, thinking about it, "it's hard to listen and to do as we're told all the time."

"And learning lessons at school is hard sometimes, too," said Alexander. "Just like your job."

Babar sat down to think about this. "Hmmm," he said. "I don't remember lessons being hard.  They were fun, as I remember."

"They are fun," said Pom. "But also serious."

"Not all fun and games," Alexander agreed. "You just don't remember that part."

"I have an idea," said Babar. "Why don't I go to school with you tomorrow. Then maybe I will be reminded."

"Great idea!" said Flora. "Maybe we could try your job some-time, too."

"Maybe," said Babar.

The next morning, when the red school bus came to pick up Pom, Flora, and Alexander, Babar got on too.

"Is it always this loud on the bus?" Babar asked, holding his ears.

"Every day," said Pom.

When they got to school, the Old Lady was waiting for them outside. Arthur was there already.

"Line up, everyone!" she said, clapping her hands. "Oh, Babar, how nice to see you! Line up a little straighter, please," she said.

In the classroom, the first part of the day was circle time, when the class talked about what they had done yesterday and what they would do today. Arthur sat next to Babar.

"Today," said the Old Lady, "we will be learning all about water."

"What did she say?" Arthur, who had just sneezed, whispered to Babar.

"She said," Babar whispered back, "that we will be learning about water."

"No talking to your neighbor during circle time, please, Babar," said the Old Lady.

After circle time it was time for reading and writing. Babar began to write a story, but his pencil broke.

The Old Lady gave him another one, but that one broke, too.

"May I have another one, please?" Babar asked her.

"All right," she said. "But that's the last one I can give you."

Next came time for arithmetic. "Who can add these two numbers together?" asked the Old Lady, writing them on the board.

"I can, I can!" said Babar. "The answer is 22."

"That was a very good try, Babar," she said. "Can anyone else give me the answer?"

"It's 32," said Flora.

Babar was embarrassed. He had forgotten to carry the one.

Finally it was time for lunch. Babar got in line with the children.

"Hmm," he said, looking at the choices. "Everything looks pretty good." He tried to decide what to have.

"You'll have to move a little faster," said the lunch lady. "The line is backed up."

Babar decided on a peanut butter sandwich and juice. He sat down at a table with the children. Then he jumped up. "Ick! What's that on my seat?" he said.

"Looks like old gum," said Pom, inspecting it.

"Or maybe very old chocolate pudding," said Arthur.

"Too sticky," said Pom. "Definitely gum."

After lunch, the class talked about water and did experiments. Babar got quite wet, but he had a very good time. He even learned a few things he did not know.

Before he knew it, it was time to go home. "I hope we'll see you tomorrow," said the Old Lady. "Please bring a good supply of pencils for yourself."

"I'm just here for today," Babar told her. "Thank you very much for having me."

The trip home on the bus was just as noisy as the trip to school.

Celeste was waiting for them when they got home. "Well, how was your day?" she asked Babar as the children ran off to get a snack.

Babar sat down on the sofa. "I am very, very tired," he said. "I think I'll go back to being a grown-up tomorrow. It's a much easier job for me."

Library of Congress Cataloging-in-Publication Data

Brunhoff, Laurent de, 1925-
  Babar goes to school / Laurent de Brunhoff.
      p. cm.
Summary: Babar has forgotten how hard it is to be a child, so he attends
grade school for a day with Pom, Flora, Isabelle, and Alexander.
  ISBN 13: 978-0-8109-4582-1
  ISBN 10: 0-8109-4582-7
  [1. Elephants—Fiction. 2. Parent and child—Fiction. 3.
Schools—Fiction. 4. Kings, queens, rulers, etc.—Fiction.] I. Title.

  PZ7.B82843Baakk 2003
  [E]—dc21
                                    2003001441

Book design by Becky Terhune

Printed and bound in China
10 9 8 7 6 5 4 3

**HNA**
**harry n. abrams, inc.**
a subsidiary of La Martinière Groupe
115 West 18th Street
New York, NY 10011
www.hnabooks.com